Dragon

Dragons are legend... n
the myths of vai
These majestic be
massive, fire-breat ...with leathery
wings and sharp claws. Dragons are associated
with great power, wisdom, and cunning.
In Western folklore, they are often depicted as
fearsome adversaries that guard valuable
treasures.
Conversely, in Eastern cultures, dragons are seen
as benevolent and bringers of good luck. The
image of dragons continues to captivate human
imagination, inspiring countless tales and works
of fantasy literature and art.

Griffin

The griffin, also known as a griffon or gryphon, is a mythical creature with the body of a lion and the head of an eagle.

This unique hybrid represents the unity of strength and keen perception, as it combines the king of beasts and the ruler of the sky.

Griffins are often portrayed as protectors of valuable treasures and divine beings, symbolizing nobility and courage.

Their image has been used throughout history as symbols of guardianship and divine power.

Unicorn

The unicorn is a legendary horse-like creature
with a single, spiraling horn on its forehead.
Revered for its beauty and purity,
the unicorn has been an enduring symbol of
innocence and magic.
In various cultures, the unicorn has been believed
to possess healing properties, and its horn was
thought to be an antidote for poisons.
Often depicted as elusive and untamed, the
unicorn has fascinated people throughout
history, leading to its appearance in numerous
myths and medieval artworks.

Phoenix

The phoenix is a mythical bird associated with resurrection and immortality.

According to legend, this magnificent creature would burst into flames and turn to ashes upon its death, only to be reborn from those very ashes. This cyclical nature of birth, death, and rebirth has made the phoenix a symbol of eternal life and renewal.

Its vivid plumage and radiant presence have inspired awe and admiration in cultures worldwide, representing hope and endurance in the face of adversity. The phoenix's story continues to be retold in various tales, inspiring hope and emphasizing the cyclical nature of life.

Hippogriff

The hippogriff is a fantastical creature that combines the body of a horse with the wings and talons of an eagle. This hybrid creature possesses both the strength and speed of a horse, along with the ability to soar through the skies with grace and agility. Known for its noble and loyal nature, the hippogriff has been featured in numerous medieval legends and stories.

It symbolizes the harmonious blending of different strengths and qualities, highlighting the importance of balance and unity in life. The hippogriff's enchanting image has made it a popular subject in fantasy art and literature, capturing the imagination of many.

Centaur

Centaurs are mythical beings with the upper body of a human and the lower body of a horse. Often depicted as skilled archers and warriors, they possess great physical strength and horse-like speed. In Greek mythology, centaurs were known for their wild and untamed behavior, reflecting the dual nature of human instincts. The portrayal of centaurs has evolved over time, representing various themes, including the struggle between civilization and savagery, and the delicate balance between human and animal instincts. Their intriguing duality continues to spark philosophical debates and creative interpretations.

Chimera

The chimera is a fearsome mythical creature that blends various animal features into one fantastical being.

Typically, it has the body of a lion, the head of a goat sprouting from its back, and a serpent's tail.

This composite beast embodies chaos and monstrosity, often serving as a symbol of destruction and unnatural power.

In mythology, the chimera was a formidable opponent, challenging heroes with its ferocity.

The concept of the chimera has persisted in literature and art, representing the complexity of the human psyche and the struggles against inner demons and vices. ,

Minotaur

The Minotaur is a mythical creature with the body of a human and the head of a bull. Condemned to live in the Labyrinth, a vast maze, the Minotaur was a terrifying and ferocious being.
This legendary figure originated from Greek mythology, representing the violent consequences of unchecked desires and the challenge of confronting one's inner darkness.
The Minotaur's story has been a subject of fascination in various art forms, exploring themes of guilt, redemption, and the human struggle to face and conquer the beast within.

Kraken

The kraken is a colossal sea monster from Nordic and Scandinavian folklore.

Often described as a giant octopus or squid, this mythical creature is said to dwell in the depths of the ocean.

Legend has it that the kraken emerges from the sea to pull entire ships underwater, leaving sailors in fear and awe of its immense power.

The kraken's mysterious presence has inspired numerous stories and serves as a cautionary tale of the unpredictable forces of the sea.

Basilisk

The basilisk is a creature of dread, known as the "king of serpents." Its mere gaze is said to be lethal, and its venom can kill with a single touch. Often depicted as a serpent or lizard with a crown-like crest on its head, the basilisk has been a symbol of fear and danger throughout history. In medieval folklore, it was believed that the basilisk could be defeated by the scent of a weasel or the reflection of itself in a mirror. This monstrous being continues to feature in tales of dark magic and perilous encounters.

Cerberus

Cerberus is a three-headed dog, a fearsome guardian of the Underworld in Greek mythology. Tasked with preventing the living from entering and the dead from escaping, Cerberus represents the boundary between life and death.

The capture of Cerberus was one of the labors of Hercules, showcasing the hero's bravery and strength. This iconic mythical creature symbolizes the passage into the afterlife and the inevitable journey we all must take.

Cerberus' imposing presence continues to inspire stories of courage and determination in the face of daunting challenges.

Pegasus

Pegasus is a winged horse in Greek mythology, born from the decapitated neck of the Gorgon Medusa.
Known for its extraordinary swiftness and ability to fly, Pegasus became the loyal companion of the hero Bellerophon.
The image of Pegasus soaring through the sky has captured the human imagination, representing freedom, inspiration, and the pursuit of dreams.
Pegasus remains an enduring symbol of hope and aspiration, reminding us that even the most audacious dreams can take flight.

Harpy

Harpies are mythical winged creatures, often depicted as female figures with the bodies of birds. In Greek mythology, they were spirits of sudden, violent winds and were considered agents of divine punishment.

Harpies were known for their ravenous hunger and would steal food from people, tormenting those they encountered. The harpies' portrayal evolved over time, representing vengeful forces, as well as the chaotic aspects of nature.

Their enigmatic existence continues to inspire interpretations of the complexities of fate and the inevitable consequences of actions.

Roc

The Roc is a colossal bird of prey originating from Arabian mythology. It is said to be so massive that it can carry off elephants in its talons.
The Roc is believed to nest on a far-off mountain and is often associated with distant, unreachable lands. The legend of the Roc has captivated explorers and adventurers throughout history, inspiring journeys to seek out mythical lands and mysterious creatures.
This majestic bird symbolizes the allure of the unknown and the quest for discovery.

Yeti

Also known as the "Abominable Snowman," the Yeti is a mythical ape-like creature said to inhabit the Himalayan mountains.

Reports of sightings and alleged footprints have sparked enduring debates about its existence.

The Yeti has become a significant figure in cryptozoology, the study of hidden or unknown animals. Its legend has become intertwined with the cultural heritage of the Himalayan region, where it remains a symbol of mystery and wilderness.

The Yeti continues to be a subject of fascination for adventurers and enthusiasts seeking to unravel the enigma of this elusive creature.

Gorgon

Gorgons are terrifying female creatures from Greek mythology, with snakes for hair and the ability to turn anyone who looked at them into stone. Medusa, the most famous Gorgon, met her end at the hands of Perseus, who used a mirror to avoid her deadly gaze.

The Gorgons embody the dark and monstrous aspects of femininity and have been interpreted as symbols of female power and the fear of the unknown. Their fearsome appearance continues to captivate artists and writers, inspiring imaginative depictions of ancient myths and allegorical tales.

Manticore

The Manticore is a legendary creature with a lion's body, a human-like face, and a tail with venomous spines.

Originating from Persian mythology, this ferocious beast was believed to be a formidable predator. The Manticore's name comes from the Greek words "manikos" (meaning "man-eater") and "thēr" (meaning "wild animal").

Throughout history, the Manticore has been a symbol of danger and the unbridled forces of nature. Its fearsome image has appeared in various cultural and artistic representations, reflecting the fascination with mythical creatures that challenge the boundaries of reality.

Nymph

Nymphs are female nature spirits found in Greek and Roman mythology. They are closely associated with natural landscapes, such as forests, rivers, and springs. Nymphs are depicted as beautiful, youthful maidens exuding grace and charm. Each type of nymph has a specific role, such as the Dryads, who are tree nymphs, and the Naiads, who inhabit bodies of water. Nymphs were believed to possess immortality, with some stories recounting love affairs between nymphs and gods or mortal heroes. The nymphs' ethereal presence continues to inspire artistic depictions of nature's allure and the connection between humans and the environment.

Siren

Sirens are enchanting creatures from Greek mythology, often depicted as beautiful women with the wings of birds.
With their mesmerizing voices, they lured sailors to their doom by singing irresistible songs, leading ships to crash upon rocky shores.
The Sirens symbolize the allure of temptation and the danger of succumbing to one's desires without regard for consequences. Their mythical songs serve as a cautionary tale about the perils of indulgence and recklessness. The legend of the Sirens has inspired numerous literary works and remains a reminder of the timeless allure of temptation and the dangers it can pose.

Werewolf

Werewolves are mythical creatures with the ability to transform from human to wolf form, often during full moons.

This legendary phenomenon, known as lycanthropy, has fascinated cultures worldwide, resulting in various werewolf myths and folklore.

The concept of werewolves has been associated with themes of primal instincts, the struggle between humanity and animalistic nature, and the terror of the unknown.

These shape-shifting creatures continue to appear in popular culture, representing the enigmatic bond between humans and the wild, untamed world of nature.

Faun

Fauns are mythical creatures that appear in Roman mythology, similar to the Greek Satyrs. They are depicted as half-human, half-goat beings, often playing musical instruments and reveling in the joy of life. Fauns are considered the guardians of nature and are associated with fertility and the changing seasons. These whimsical creatures embody the joyful and carefree aspects of life, encouraging people to connect with nature's rhythms and embrace the pleasures of existence. Fauns' imagery has influenced art, literature, and music, inspiring expressions of jubilant creativity and appreciation for the natural world.

Selkie

Selkies are mythical beings found in Celtic folklore, particularly in the traditions of Ireland, Scotland, and the Faroe Islands. Selkies are seals capable of shedding their skin and transforming into beautiful humans. Legend has it that when a selkie comes ashore and dons its human form, it can enchant those who witness its grace and beauty. Selkies are often featured in tales of love, as humans form bonds with these creatures, leading to separations when the selkie returns to its oceanic home. The story of the selkie serves as an enduring reminder of the transient nature of love and the profound connection between humans and the natural world.

Kitsune

Kitsune are mythical fox spirits from Japanese folklore. They possess intelligence, magical abilities, and the power to shape-shift into human form. In some tales, kitsune are benevolent and act as protectors or bringers of good fortune.

In others, they may be mischievous or even malevolent, using their shape-shifting abilities to deceive or manipulate humans.

Kitsune are often associated with Inari, the Shinto god of rice and fertility.

The multi-faceted nature of kitsune reflects the complexities of human emotions and serves as a reminder of the dualities within us all.

Kelpie

Kelpies are mythical water spirits originating from Scottish and Irish folklore.
They are often portrayed as shape-shifting horses or water horses that lure unsuspecting travelers into water bodies, then dragging them under to their watery demise.
Kelpies are considered malevolent beings, symbolizing the dangerous allure of the unknown and the unpredictability of nature.
Tales of kelpies serve as cautionary warnings about the perils of the water and the need for caution when navigating the treacherous currents of life.

Thunderbird

The Thunderbird is a mythical creature from various Native American cultures, particularly among indigenous peoples of the Great Plains and the Pacific Northwest. It is a powerful and majestic bird that controls the forces of thunder and lightning. Thunderbirds are often associated with natural phenomena, such as storms and rain, and are considered sacred beings with great spiritual significance. Thunderbirds play a central role in creation stories and are seen as protectors of the earth and its inhabitants. Its majestic presence represents the awe-inspiring forces of nature and the spiritual connections between humans and the natural world.

Jackalope

The jackalope is a mythical creature from North American folklore, particularly in the western United States.
It is said to be a combination of a jackrabbit and an antelope, with the distinctive feature of having antlers on its head.
The legend of the jackalope has evolved into a playful tale, with humorous accounts of sightings and attempts to catch this elusive creature.
The jackalope serves as a lighthearted reminder of the joys of storytelling and the enduring tradition of sharing fantastical tales in local communities.

Chupacabra

The Chupacabra is a legendary creature from Latin American folklore, particularly in Puerto Rico and Mexico. Its name translates to "goat-sucker," as it is said to attack and feed on livestock, particularly goats. Descriptions of the Chupacabra vary, with some accounts depicting it as a reptilian creature, while others describe it as a fearsome, vampire-like beast. Sightings of the Chupacabra have sparked fear and intrigue in local communities, leading to various cultural interpretations and media portrayals of this mysterious cryptid. The legend of the Chupacabra continues to intrigue and captivate those fascinated by cryptids and urban legends.

Bunyip

The Bunyip is a mythical creature from Aboriginal Australian folklore. It is believed to inhabit water bodies such as rivers, swamps, and billabongs. Descriptions of the Bunyip vary among different Aboriginal cultures, but it is often depicted as a fearsome, large creature with a mix of animal features, such as a dog-like face, flippers, and tusks. The Bunyip's legend served as an important aspect of traditional storytelling, emphasizing the significance of respecting and understanding the natural environment. The Bunyip continues to hold cultural importance as a symbol of the enduring connection between Aboriginal communities and the land.

Wendigo

The Wendigo is a terrifying creature from Algonquian folklore, prevalent among indigenous peoples in the northern United States and Canada.
It is depicted as a cannibalistic, gaunt figure with an insatiable hunger for human flesh.
The Wendigo is believed to be the result of a person giving in to their darkest impulses and resorting to cannibalism during extreme conditions.
The legend of the Wendigo serves as a cautionary tale about the dangers of greed, selfishness, and the destructive consequences of surrendering to our innermost fears and desires.

Nemean Lion

The Nemean Lion is a formidable creature from Greek mythology, known for its invulnerable hide and immense strength.

According to legend, Hercules was tasked with slaying the Nemean Lion as part of his Twelve Labors. The lion's impenetrable hide made it immune to most weapons, leading Hercules to use his bare hands to strangle the beast.

The Nemean Lion's defeat symbolizes the triumph of courage and resourcefulness over seemingly insurmountable challenges. This legendary creature continues to inspire depictions of bravery and the quest for heroism in the face of adversity.

Baku

The Baku is a mythical creature from Japanese folklore, often described as a benevolent spirit with the appearance of a chimera, combining elements of elephants, tigers, and bears.
The Baku is believed to possess the power to devour and dispel nightmares. In times of trouble or bad dreams, people call upon the Baku for protection and to rid them of their distressing visions. The Baku's legend has woven its way into popular culture, becoming a symbol of hope and comfort in the face of fear and anxiety.
Its protective presence continues to be invoked in various forms of art and literature as a symbol of relief and peace of mind.

Qilin

The Qilin, also known as the Chinese unicorn, is a mythical creature from Chinese mythology.
It is a gentle and benevolent being, considered to be an auspicious omen and a symbol of peace and prosperity. The Qilin's appearance is a combination of various animals, featuring the body of a deer, the tail of an ox, and hooves like a horse. Its kind nature has led to it being associated with wise rulers and the arrival of great leaders or benevolent eras. The Qilin's imagery remains an iconic symbol of harmony and good fortune in Chinese culture, inspiring artistic depictions and representations in various forms of traditional and contemporary art.

Hippocampus

The Hippocampus is a mythical sea creature from Greek mythology, combining the upper body of a horse with the tail of a fish. These graceful beings are often depicted as the companions of sea deities and were considered the embodiment of strength and elegance. In ancient times, seafarers believed that the presence of Hippocampi indicated safe and bountiful voyages.

The Hippocampus symbolizes the powerful connection between land and sea, reflecting the mysteries and wonders of the ocean. Its imagery continues to inspire contemporary art and represents the allure of exploring the vast depths of the aquatic realm.

Simurgh

The Simurgh is a mythical bird from Persian mythology, often compared to the phoenix and the griffin. This majestic creature is believed to be benevolent, wise, and immensely powerful. The Simurgh is said to have healing powers, bringing relief to those who seek its aid. Additionally, it serves as a symbol of purity, divinity, and spiritual transformation. The Simurgh's name translates to "30 birds," representing its mystical connection to the number 30, a symbol of renewal and rebirth. The Simurgh continues to be celebrated in Persian culture, inspiring artistic interpretations of its radiant and compassionate nature.

Leviathan

Leviathan is a colossal sea monster from various mythologies, including ancient Near Eastern and Hebrew traditions. It is often described as a massive, multi-headed serpent or dragon, representing the untamed forces of the ocean. Leviathan embodies chaos, and its defeat symbolizes the triumph of order and divine power over chaos and destruction.

The concept of Leviathan has been interpreted in various ways, serving as a metaphor for the challenges of life and the need to confront the unknown with courage and faith. The imagery of Leviathan reflects humanity's fascination with the mysteries and perils of the deep sea.

Golem

The Golem is a legendary creature from Jewish folklore, originating from the Kabbalistic tradition. It is an artificial being, usually created from clay and brought to life through mystical rituals. Golems are depicted as powerful, loyal protectors, acting on the commands of their creators. However, the creation of a Golem can also lead to unintended consequences, raising ethical questions about humanity's role as a creator and the responsibilities that come with such power. The legend of the Golem serves as a poignant reminder of the potential dangers and moral dilemmas associated with creating artificial life.

Jormungandr

Jormungandr, also known as the Midgard Serpent, is a massive sea serpent from Norse mythology. According to legend, Jormungandr encircles the world, holding its tail in its mouth, and its thrashing movements cause violent storms and tidal waves. In the Norse cosmology, Jormungandr is one of Loki's offspring and plays a pivotal role in the events leading to Ragnarok, the apocalyptic battle that marks the end of the world. The image of Jormungandr as an immense serpent embodying the forces of chaos and destruction continues to be a powerful symbol in Norse culture, representing the cyclical nature of life and the inevitability of cosmic events.

Peryton

The Peryton is a mythical creature that combines the features of a deer with the wings of a bird of prey, often depicted as a majestic, albeit eerie, creature. According to legend, Perytons cast the shadows of human beings while flying overhead. These unique beings have been associated with various symbolism, such as the pursuit of unattainable ideals and the boundary between the human and animal worlds.

The Peryton's enigmatic presence continues to inspire interpretations in art, literature, and popular culture, as it represents the uncanny blending of disparate elements, both graceful and haunting.

Chimaera

The Chimaera is a fearsome creature from Greek mythology, with the head of a lion, the body of a goat, and the tail of a serpent. It was a monstrous offspring of Typhon and Echidna, a pair of monstrous beings themselves. The Chimaera was known for terrorizing the land of Lycia, causing destruction and fear among its inhabitants. This legendary creature symbolizes the embodiment of malevolent forces and represents the constant struggle between civilization and the untamed wilderness. Its fearsome appearance has made it a popular subject in ancient art and continues to inspire interpretations exploring the complexities of good versus evil.

Lamassu

The Lamassu is a protective deity from ancient Mesopotamian mythology, particularly associated with the Assyrian civilization.
This majestic creature has the body of a bull or lion, the wings of an eagle, and the head of a human.
Lamassus were believed to guard the entrances to palaces, temples, and cities, protecting their inhabitants from evil spirits and malevolent forces. These guardian spirits represent the melding of human intelligence and animal strength, embodying the idea of divine protection and the bond between the earthly and divine realms.

Vampire

Vampires are legendary creatures often depicted as undead beings that subsist on the blood of the living. Originating from various folklore traditions, vampires have become iconic figures in popular culture. The image of the vampire has evolved over time, from malevolent, shape-shifting demons to charming, tormented immortals. Legends about vampires have spread across the globe, with each culture adding its own unique twist to the myth. Their enduring popularity is a testament to humanity's fascination with the enigmatic, eternal, and alluring aspects of these nocturnal creatures.

Banshee

Banshees are eerie female spirits from Irish folklore, known for their haunting wails that foretell impending death.
They serve as harbingers of doom and mournful omens for families.
Legends say their cries echo through the night, a chilling reminder of mortality.
Banshees represent the fear of death and the mystery surrounding the afterlife in Celtic mythology.
The keen, sorrowful cries of the banshee continue to captivate imaginations and inspire tales of the supernatural.

Wyvern

Wyverns are dragon-like creatures with two legs, wings, and venomous fangs.
They inhabit ancient ruins and guard valuable treasures. While not as well-known as dragons, wyverns are equally formidable and feared in medieval folklore.
Wyverns' reptilian features make them symbols of power, cunning, and the unknown.
Their lore continues to influence fantasy literature and heraldry, embodying the allure of the mythical and enigmatic.

Hydra

The Hydra is a fearsome serpent-like creature from Greek mythology, possessing regenerative abilities.
When one of its many heads is severed, two more grow in its place. This makes the Hydra nearly invincible, a formidable challenge for heroes like Hercules.
The Hydra's symbolism lies in the idea that confronting one problem may lead to the emergence of more. The myth of the Hydra serves as a reminder of the complexities of life and the need to address root causes rather than symptoms.

Gargoyle

Gargoyles are stone creatures that perch on buildings, serving as protectors and warding off evil spirits.

In medieval architecture, they were believed to come to life at night to guard the structures they adorned. Gargoyles represent the battle between good and evil, as their presence protects against malevolent forces.

The grotesque and eerie appearance of gargoyles adds an air of mystery and symbolism to the architectural wonders of ancient structures.

Tengu

Tengu are mythical creatures from Japanese folklore, depicted as bird-like beings with long noses. They possess martial skills and are often considered both protectors and tricksters.
Tengu symbolize the duality of nature, embodying both benevolence and mischief. They serve as guardians of the mountains and forests, reflecting the Japanese reverence for nature and its powerful forces.
The enigmatic nature of Tengu continues to inspire creativity in Japanese art, theater, and storytelling.

Naga

Nagas are serpent-like beings found in Hindu, Buddhist, and Southeast Asian folklore.
They are associated with water, fertility, and transformation. Nagas can be both benevolent and malevolent, representing the duality of existence.
In many cultures, Nagas hold significant religious importance, with legends attributing their ancestry to powerful deities. Nagas' symbolism reflects the interconnectedness of life, cycles of renewal, and the deep respect for the natural world.

Slender Man

Slender Man is a modern internet-born mythical creature, portrayed as a tall, thin figure with a featureless face.

Created as an internet meme, Slender Man's horror stories and urban legends spread rapidly, captivating the imaginations of many.

He embodies the fear of the unknown and the power of digital storytelling in shaping contemporary folklore.

Slender Man's cultural impact is a testament to the enduring allure of creating and sharing modern myths in the digital age.

Valkyrie

Valkyries are mythical female figures from Norse mythology, associated with war and choosing fallen warriors for Valhalla.
As choosers of the slain, they play a significant role in Norse afterlife beliefs.
Valkyries exemplify courage and valor, inspiring warriors to face death fearlessly.
Their image continues to be a symbol of powerful and fierce women, highlighting their central role in Norse mythology and the appreciation of strong female figures in Viking culture.

Mermaid

Mermaids are enchanting beings with the upper body of a human and the lower body of a fish. Their allure lies in the beauty, grace, and mystique of the ocean.

Legends of mermaids can be found in cultures worldwide, symbolizing the irresistible pull of the sea and the unknown depths.

Mermaids represent a longing for freedom and escape from the constraints of earthly existence. Their captivating charm continues to inspire art, literature, and a sense of wonder for the vastness of the ocean.

Cyclops

Cyclopes are one-eyed giants from Greek mythology, known for their immense strength. The most famous Cyclops, Polyphemus, appeared in Homer's "Odyssey," where he confronted Odysseus and his crew.

Cyclopes embody the theme of isolation and the limitations of perception. In contrast to their ferocity, some myths depict Cyclopes as skilled craftsmen, creating thunderbolts for the gods. Their portrayal in ancient literature and art has left an enduring impact on the depiction of giants in mythology.

Sphinx

The Sphinx is a mystical creature from Egyptian mythology, having the body of a lion and the head of a human.

It guards the entrance to a tomb and poses riddles to travelers. The most famous Sphinx appears in the myth of Oedipus, challenging him with a riddle.

Sphinxes symbolize mystery, wisdom, and the enigmatic nature of life's questions.

Their imposing presence continues to intrigue and inspire philosophical reflections on the human condition.

Wraith

Wraiths are malevolent spirits or ghosts from various cultures, associated with death and haunting the living.

They are often depicted as shadowy figures or specters. Wraiths embody the fear of death, the unknown, and the unresolved aspects of the human experience.

Stories of wraiths have persisted across cultures, reflecting a universal fascination with the afterlife and the mysteries beyond our understanding.

Wraiths' haunting presence serves as a reminder of the impermanence of life and the mysteries of the beyond.

Kappa

Kappa is a mischievous water imp from Japanese folklore, known for its love of cucumbers and sumo wrestling.
Despite their playful nature, Kappas can be dangerous and may drown humans or livestock in rivers.
Kappa legends emphasize the importance of respecting water bodies and safety around them.
Kappas' captivating blend of charm and mischief has made them popular subjects in Japanese art, literature, and modern popular culture.

Jinn

Jinn, also known as genies, are supernatural beings from Islamic mythology capable of granting wishes.

However, they are not always benevolent and may trick or deceive those who encounter them.

Jinn embody the mysterious and unpredictable aspects of the unseen world.

In Islamic lore, they are created from smokeless fire and exist alongside humans, influencing destinies and choices.

Jinn continue to inspire tales of magic and wonder, exploring the interplay between humanity and the ethereal realm.

Bigfoot

Bigfoot, also known as Sasquatch, is a legendary ape-like creature believed to inhabit remote forests, particularly in North America. Descriptions of Bigfoot vary, but it's generally portrayed as a tall, hairy, and elusive being. Sightings and footprints have fueled speculation about this creature, making it a prominent figure in North American folklore and cryptozoology. The mystery surrounding Bigfoot continues to inspire curiosity and exploration, with numerous researchers and enthusiasts seeking to unravel the truth behind this mythical giant. Tales of Bigfoot have become ingrained in popular culture, inspiring all sorts of media.

Krampus

Krampus is a mythical creature from Central European folklore, known as the dark counterpart to St. Nicholas.

During the Christmas season, while St. Nicholas rewards well-behaved children with gifts, Krampus punishes the misbehaving ones. With its terrifying appearance, typically depicted as a horned, hairy demon, and folklore customs that include parades and festivals, Krampus serves as a cautionary tale for children to behave and appreciate the spirit of the holiday season. The tradition of Krampus has experienced a resurgence in recent years, gaining popularity beyond its European origins.

Mummie

Mummies are preserved corpses, often wrapped in bandages, from ancient cultures such as Egypt, where elaborate rituals were performed to prepare the deceased for the afterlife.

These ancient funerary practices aimed to ensure the continuity of life after death, believing in an eternal journey in the afterworld.

Legends of cursed mummies coming back to life have inspired numerous horror stories and movies, contributing to the enduring allure of mummies in popular culture.

The mystery and fascination with mummies also extend to the study of archaeology and anthropology.

Loch Ness Monster

The Loch Ness Monster, affectionately known as Nessie, is a mythical aquatic creature said to inhabit Scotland's Loch Ness, one of the largest and deepest freshwater lochs in the UK. Descriptions of Nessie vary, but it's often depicted as a large, long-necked creature resembling a plesiosaur. The legend of the Loch Ness Monster dates back centuries, with sightings and alleged photographs creating a sensation that has endured through the years. The mystery of Nessie has become an integral part of Scottish folklore and tourism, attracting visitors from around the world eager to catch a glimpse of this enigmatic creature.

Jersey Devil

The Jersey Devil is a legendary creature said to haunt the Pine Barrens of New Jersey, USA. Descriptions of the Jersey Devil vary, but it's often portrayed as a flying, hooved creature with a goat's head and bat-like wings.

The legend of the Jersey Devil has been passed down for generations, contributing to the folklore of the region and inspiring numerous urban legends and tales of the supernatural. Sightings and encounters have been reported over the years, and the legend remains a significant part of New Jersey's cultural heritage.

Changeling

Changelings are mythical creatures from European folklore, believed to be fairy children swapped with human infants.

Tales of changelings reflect the fears surrounding infant mortality and the need to explain developmental disorders or sudden changes in behavior. In these legends, fairies or other supernatural beings would secretly replace a human child with a changeling, leading to tales of misfortune and mysterious occurrences.

These stories served as cautionary tales to young children and fascinated communities with the possibility of supernatural beings living among them.

Mothman

Mothman is a creature from American folklore, famously associated with sightings in Point Pleasant, West Virginia, in the 1960s. Descriptions of Mothman vary, but it's often described as a winged humanoid with glowing red eyes.

The Mothman sightings created a sensation and have become an enduring mystery in paranormal lore, attracting enthusiasts and inspiring books, films, and local festivals.

While the origin of the Mothman sightings remains a subject of debate, the legend has become an integral part of Point Pleasant's identity, and the town embraces the creature as a unique and fascinating aspect of its history.

Skinwalker

Skinwalkers are mythical beings from Navajo mythology, believed to be witches or shapeshifters capable of transforming into animals.

In Navajo culture, the concept of skinwalkers holds significant spiritual and cultural importance, associated with dark practices and malevolent intent. Stories of skinwalkers have been passed down through generations, representing the fear of the unknown and the dangers that lie in the spiritual world.

The topic of skinwalkers is treated with sensitivity and respect, as it is considered sacred knowledge within the Navajo community.

Oni

Oni are supernatural creatures from Japanese folklore, often depicted as fearsome demons with horns and wild hair. Despite their intimidating appearance, some Oni are benevolent, while others are mischievous or malevolent.
They feature prominently in Japanese art, theater, and festivals, symbolizing the balance of good and evil in the world.
Oni are deeply rooted in Japanese culture, and their presence extends beyond the realm of folklore. They are a symbol of human desires, representing the internal struggle between good intentions and negative impulses.

Ogre

Ogres are monstrous beings found in various cultural myths, known for their immense size and strength.Often portrayed as dim-witted or fearsome, they play roles as both villains and helpers in fairy tales and folklore. Ogres' tales explore themes of bravery and wit, teaching valuable lessons to children about inner strength and resilience. These legendary creatures have become enduring figures in literature and popular culture, demonstrating that appearances can be deceiving and highlighting the importance of empathy and understanding.

In folklore, ogres represent the fear of the unknown and the challenges we encounter in life.

Leprechaun

Leprechauns are small, mischievous creatures from Irish folklore, famous for their love of gold and hidden treasure. Legends say that if you catch a leprechaun, it will grant you three wishes in exchange for its freedom.

These elusive beings continue to enchant the world with their tales of magic and pots of gold at the end of rainbows. The mischievous nature of leprechauns has become synonymous with playful trickery, evoking laughter and wonder in the hearts of both children and adults. Beyond their iconic appearance in St. Patrick's Day celebrations, leprechauns have become enduring symbols of Ireland's rich cultural heritage.

Gnome

Gnomes are diminutive creatures found in European folklore, often associated with gardens and natural spaces.

They are known for their affinity for nature, craftsmanship, and benevolence toward humans.

Gnomes have become beloved figures in literature and popular culture, adding a touch of whimsy and charm to our imaginations.

The gentle and nurturing nature of gnomes has made them popular symbols of protection and good luck, believed to bring blessings to gardens and homes. Their stories inspire a sense of connection to the natural world, encouraging harmony with the environment.

Goblin

Goblins are small, mischievous beings from various mythologies, known for their trickster nature and penchant for causing trouble. While some goblins are playful, others can be malevolent. They have appeared in stories around the world, serving as cautionary tales about the consequences of greed and deceit. In folklore, goblins embody the unpredictable and chaotic aspects of life, often challenging the order and complacency of society. Their stories serve as warnings against the lure of material desires and the dangers of indulging in destructive behaviors. Despite their reputation for mischief, some goblins also possess wisdom and wit.

Fairy

Fairies are ethereal beings from folklore, often depicted as delicate, winged creatures with magical powers. They are associated with nature, beauty, and enchantment. Stories of fairies have captivated imaginations for generations, weaving tales of wonder and the supernatural. In various cultural traditions, fairies have been celebrated as guardians of the natural world, protectors of sacred places, and emissaries of both light and darkness. Their stories inspire a sense of wonder and curiosity, inviting us to explore the mystical aspects of our surroundings. The captivating allure of fairies lies in the idea that magical realms might exist just beyond our perception.

Aqrabuamelu

Aqrabuamelu, also known as the Scorpion Men, are mythical creatures from Mesopotamian mythology. They are depicted as half-human, half-scorpion beings, guarding the gates of the underworld. Aqrabuamelu represent the duality of nature and serve as gatekeepers between life and death. In ancient Mesopotamian belief, these enigmatic beings were seen as powerful protectors, standing as fierce and loyal sentinels at the threshold of the underworld.

Their role as guardians of the afterlife highlights the ancient Mesopotamians' fascination with the mysteries of existence and the transition from one state of being to another.

Zombie

Zombies are reanimated corpses from Haitian and Caribbean folklore, often associated with voodoo practices.

These undead beings are popular figures in horror and pop culture, symbolizing fear of death, loss of control, and the consequences of tampering with the natural order.

The notion of zombies has evolved significantly from their Haitian origins to become a prevalent theme in modern literature, movies, and video games.

In contemporary fiction, zombies represent societal anxieties, such as pandemics, consumerism, and the loss of identity.

Pontianak

Pontianak is a female vampire-like creature from Southeast Asian folklore, believed to be the spirit of a woman who died while pregnant.
She haunts the night, seeking revenge or justice for her untimely death. Legends of the Pontianak have been passed down through generations, cautioning against disrespecting women and the consequences of violence.
In Southeast Asian cultures, the tale of the Pontianak serves as a reminder of the importance of respecting women's rights and the consequences of mistreatment and oppression. As a vengeful spirit, the Pontianak embodies the idea that actions have consequences.

Bogeyman

The Bogeyman is a mythical creature found in various cultures, known for scaring misbehaving children into good behavior. It embodies the fear of the unknown and serves as a reminder of the consequences of disobedience.

The Bogeyman has taken on different forms in different cultures, reflecting the diversity of human fears. The concept of the Bogeyman speaks to the universal experience of childhood anxieties and the role of storytelling in teaching moral lessons.

Tales of the Bogeyman have been used as a tool for instilling discipline and reinforcing social norms across cultures.

Dybbuk

Dybbuk is a malevolent spirit from Jewish folklore, believed to be the soul of a deceased person possessing the living.

Dybbuks are associated with tragic deaths and unfinished business, seeking resolution or revenge. These dark tales explore themes of redemption and spiritual turmoil.

In Jewish folklore, the concept of the dybbuk reflects the belief in the persistence of the soul and the potential for unresolved issues to linger beyond death. Dybbuk stories serve as cautionary tales, warning against the consequences of unfulfilled responsibilities and the importance of finding closure in life.

Poltergeist

Poltergeists are supernatural entities known for their disruptive and mischievous behavior. They are often linked to haunted houses, where objects move or noises are heard without any apparent cause. Poltergeist tales have captivated audiences in horror films, sparking the imagination about the existence of malevolent spirits. In various cultures, poltergeists are seen as manifestations of repressed emotions or psychic energy, providing a framework to understand unexplained phenomena. Poltergeist legends tap into the universal fascination with the unknown and the possibility of paranormal activity in the world around us.

Kobalin

Kobalins are mischievous household spirits from Estonian folklore, believed to live in stables or barns. They enjoy playing pranks on humans but can be appeased with offerings of food and drink. Kobalins' stories reflect the Estonian reverence for nature and their belief in the unseen world. In Estonian culture, the kobalins symbolize the interconnectedness of humans and nature, emphasizing the importance of harmony and respect for the natural environment. The tales of kobalins serve as reminders of the old traditions and customs of rural life, evoking a sense of nostalgia for a simpler time when humans lived in close communion with nature.

Dwarf

Dwarves are legendary beings found in various mythologies and folklore. Often depicted as short-statured, skilled craftsmen, and miners, dwarves are renowned for their craftsmanship and knowledge of precious metals and gems.
In Norse mythology, they forged powerful weapons and treasures for the gods, including Thor's mighty hammer, Mjölnir. Despite their modest height, dwarves are celebrated for their immense strength and resilience, which they channel into their masterful creations.
Their underground homes are said to be intricate and magnificent, reflecting their affinity for the earth and its hidden treasures.

Giant

Giants are colossal creatures of immense strength and stature, appearing in myths and legends worldwide.

Often associated with natural forces like thunderstorms, earthquakes, and volcanic eruptions, they embody the awe-inspiring power of nature and its unfathomable scale. In Norse mythology, giants played pivotal roles in shaping the world and its destiny. Jotunheim, the land of giants, stood as a realm of both wonder and peril. The clash between gods and giants exemplified the eternal struggle between order and chaos. Giants' legendary feats, from constructing megalithic structures to hurling boulders.

Elves

Elves are graceful and ethereal beings from folklore, known for their beauty, agility, and connection to nature.
They exist in various cultural traditions, each with distinct characteristics and roles.
In Norse mythology, elves were celestial creatures living in Alfheim, while in Germanic folklore, they were guardian spirits of the forest.
Elves' appearance ranges from fair-haired and ethereal to mischievous and whimsical, embodying the allure of the mysterious and the magical. Gifted with extraordinary talents, elves excel in art, music, and archery.

Fenrir

Fenrir, a monstrous wolf, is a prominent figure in Norse mythology. Prophesied to bring about Ragnarok, the end of the world, Fenrir is a symbol of chaos and destruction.

Despite Odin's efforts to bind him, Fenrir's strength grew, and he eventually broke free, setting in motion the cataclysmic events of the apocalypse. As a primal force of nature, Fenrir embodies the unstoppable and unpredictable aspects of existence. His ferocity and untamed nature underscore the inevitability of change and the cyclical nature of creation and destruction. Fenrir's legend serves as a poignant reminder of the inevitable struggle between gods and fate.

Behemoth

Behemoth is a colossal and enigmatic creature mentioned in ancient texts like the Book of Job and various religious scriptures. Described as a mighty, herbivorous beast, Behemoth symbolizes primordial power and often represents the untamable forces of nature. In some interpretations, Behemoth is associated with chaos and wilderness, while others see it as a divine being. The mystery surrounding Behemoth has made it a captivating figure in religious and mythical literature, sparking various interpretations over the ages. Behemoth's legend endures as a testament to humanity's enduring fascination with the mysteries of the world.

Adlet

Adlet, also known as Erqigdlit, are mythical creatures from Inuit mythology.
These beings have the upper body of a human and the lower body of a dog or wolf. Adlet are believed to be the result of an unnatural union between a human woman and a dog.Considered fierce hunters and warriors, they exhibit agility and strength, making them formidable adversaries in legends and tales. Adlet's unique hybrid appearance showcases the Inuit people's reverence for the bond between humans and animals, emphasizing the interconnectedness of all living beings. Adlet embody the harmony between humanity and the natural world.

Cacus

In Roman mythology, Cacus was a monstrous fire-breathing creature that terrorized ancient Italy. With a dragon-like appearance, Cacus lived in a cave on the Aventine Hill.

In the tale of Hercules' Labors, Cacus stole cattle from Hercules, leading to a dramatic confrontation. Hercules defeated Cacus, making him a symbol of the triumph of heroism over evil forces. Cacus' legend embodies the Roman value of valor and the triumph of righteousness over malevolence.

The tale serves as a reminder of the eternal struggle between good and evil, symbolizing humanity's resilience in the face of adversity.

Ammit

Ammit, also known as the Devourer of the Dead, is an ancient Egyptian mythical creature with a fearsome reputation. In the afterlife judgment, the heart of the deceased was weighed against the feather of Ma'at, the goddess of truth and justice. If the heart was heavier with sin, Ammit would consume it, preventing the soul from entering the afterlife. Ammit served as a powerful reminder of the importance of a righteous life in Egyptian beliefs. As a hybrid creature, Ammit combines the characteristics of a lion, hippopotamus, and crocodile, all of which were seen as potent symbols of death and destruction in ancient Egypt.

Printed in Dunstable, United Kingdom